WHERE THE BUFFALOES BEGIN

O L A F   B A K E R

WHERE THE BUFFALOES BEGIN

◇◆◇

Drawings by

S T E P H E N   G A M M E L L

Troll Associates

PUFFIN BOOKS
A Division of Penguin Books USA Inc.
375 Hudson Street, New York, New York 10014
Penguin Books Ltd, Harmondsworth, Middlesex, England
Penguin Books Australia Ltd, Ringwood, Victoria, Australia
Penguin Books Canada Limited, 2801 John Street, Markham, Ontario, Canada L3R 1B4
Penguin Books (N.Z.) Ltd, 182–190 Wairau Road, Auckland 10, New Zealand

First published by Frederick Warne & Co., Inc., 1981
Published in Picture Puffins 1985
10 9 8 7 6 5 4 3 2 1
Text copyright © Frederick Warne and Co., Inc., 1981
Illustrations copyright © Stephen Gammell, 1981
All rights reserved

Library of Congress catalog card number: 85-5682
(CIP data available)
ISBN 0–14-050560-1

Printed in the United States of America

Set in Caslon 540

TO MY FRIEND
RED EAGLE

Over the blazing camp-fires, when the wind moaned eerily through the thickets of juniper and fir, they spoke of it in the Indian tongue—of the strange lake to the south whose waters never rest. And Nawa, the wise man, who had lived such countless moons that not even the oldest member of the tribe could remember a time when Nawa was not old, declared that if you arrived at the right time, on the right night, you would see the buffaloes rise out of the middle of the lake and come crowding to the shore; for there, he said, was the sacred spot where the buffaloes began. It was not only Nawa who declared that the buffaloes had their beginnings beneath the water and were born in the depths of the lake. The Indian legend, far older even than Nawa, said the same thing. Nawa was only the voice that kept the legend alive.

OFTEN IN THE WINTER,
WHEN THE WIND DROVE WITH A
ROAR over the prairies and came thundering up the creek, making the tepees
shudder and strain, Little Wolf would listen to the wind and think it was the stampede
of the buffaloes. Then he would snuggle warmly under the buffalo robe that was his
blanket and would be thankful for the shelter of his home. And sometimes he would
go very far down the shadow ways of sleep and would meet the buffaloes as they came
up from the lake, with the water shining on their shaggy coats and their black horns
gleaming in the moon. And the buffaloes would begin by being very terrible, shaking
their great heads at him as if they intended to kill him there and then. But later they
would come up close, and smell him, and change their minds, and be friendly after all.

◈ Little Wolf was only ten years old, but he could run faster than any of his friends. And the wildest pony was not too wild for him to catch and ride. But the great thing about him was that he had no fear. He knew that if an angry bull bison or a pack of prairie wolves ran him down, there would be nothing left of him but his bones. And he was well aware that if he fell into the hands of his people's enemies, the Assiniboins, he would be killed and scalped as neatly as could be. Yet none of these things terrified him. Only, being wise for his age, he had a clear understanding that, for the present, it was better to keep out of their way.

◈ But of all the thoughts that ran this way and that in his quick brain, the one that galloped the hardest was the thought of the great lake to the south where the buffaloes began. And as the days lengthened and he could smell springtime on the warm blowing air, the thought grew bigger and bigger in Little Wolf's mind. At last it was so very big that Little Wolf could not bear it any longer; and so, one morning, very early, before the village was awake, he crept out of the tepee and stole along below the junipers and tall firs till he came to the spot where the ponies were hobbled.

T
HE DAWN WAS JUST BEGIN-
NING TO BREAK, AND IN THE GRAY
LIGHT the ponies looked like dark blotches along the creek. But Little Wolf's
eyes were very sharp, and soon he had singled out his own pony, because it had a white
forefoot and a white patch on its left side. When Little Wolf spoke, calling softly, the
animal whinnied in answer and allowed itself to be caught. Little Wolf unhobbled the
pony, slipped on the bridle he had brought with him, and leaped lightly upon its back.
A few minutes afterward, horse and rider had left the camp behind them and were out
on the prairie, going due south.

◈ When the sun rose, they had already traveled far. Little Wolf's eyes constantly swept the immense horizon, searching for danger, moving or in half-concealed ambush. Far off, just on the edge of his sight, there was a dim spot on the yellowish gray of the prairie. Little Wolf reined in his pony and watched to see if it moved. If it did, it crept so slowly as to seem absolutely still. He decided that it was a herd of antelope feeding and that there was nothing to fear.

◈ On he went, hour after hour, never ceasing to watch. The prairie grouse got up almost under the pony's feet. Larks and sparrows filled the air with their singing, and everywhere wild roses were in bloom. It seemed as if nothing but peace would ever find its way among these singing birds and flowers; yet Little Wolf knew well that his enemies, the Assiniboins, could come creeping along the hollows of the prairie like wolves, and that there is no moment more dangerous than when there is no hint of danger.

◈ All this time he had not seen a single buffalo, but he told himself that this was because the herds had taken some other way and that he would probably not see them until he was near the lake. He lost sight of the shadowy spot that had been so far away. If he had known that it was a party of Assiniboins on the way to his village, he would have thought twice about continuing to the lake and would probably have returned along the trail to give warning to his people. But his head was too full of the singing of birds and the breath of roses, and, above all, of the great thought of the buffaloes, fighting below the lake.

◈ It was late in the afternoon when, at last, he sighted the lake. It lay, a gray sheet with a glint of silver, glimmering under the sun. Little Wolf looked eagerly on all sides for any sign of buffaloes, but far and wide the prairies lay utterly deserted, very warm and still in the white shimmer of the air. As he drew nearer, however, he saw trails, many trails, all going in one direction and leading toward the lake. Antelope and coyote, wolf and buffalo—all had left traces behind them as they went to the water and returned. But it was the buffalo trails that were most numerous and most marked, and Little Wolf noted them above all the others.

◈ When he was quite close to the lake, he dismounted; hobbling the pony, he turned it loose to graze. Then Little Wolf lay down behind some tussocks of prairie grass, above the low bank at the edge of the lake, and waited. From this position he could overlook the lake without being seen. He gazed far over its glittering expanse, very still now under the strong beams of the sun. It was disappointingly still. Scarcely a ripple broke on the shore. Little Wolf could not possibly imagine that the buffaloes were struggling underneath. Where was the movement and the mysterious murmur of which Nawa had spoken? But Little Wolf was not impatient. He could afford to wait and listen for hours, if need be.

◈ The time went on. Slowly the sun dipped westward, and the shadows of the grass grew longer. The lake kept its outward stillness, and nothing happened. At last the sun reached the horizon; it lay there a few moments, a great ball of flame, then sank out of sight. Twilight fell, and all over the vast wilderness crept a peculiar silence, like a wild creature stealing from its lair. Far in the west there lingered the strange orange light that belongs to the prairie skies alone when the sun is down and the night

winds sigh along the grass. Little Wolf could not tell whether it was the sighing of the wind or not, but there came to him along the margin of the lake a strange, low murmur that died away and rose again. As the night deepened, the sound grew clearer; Little Wolf was certain now that it was not the wind but a murmur that came from the center of the lake. For hours he lay and listened, but the mysterious murmur never ceased. Sometimes it was a little louder, sometimes a little softer; but always it was plain to hear—a wonderful and terrible thing in the silence of the night. And as Little Wolf lay watching under the stars, the words of Nawa kept singing in his head:

Do you hear the noise that never ceases?
It is the Buffaloes fighting far below.
They are fighting to get out upon the prairie.
They are born below the Water but are fighting
      for the Air,
In the great lake in the Southland where the
      Buffaloes begin!

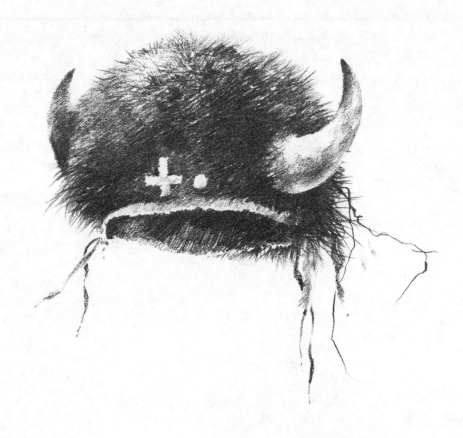

SUDDENLY LITTLE WOLF
LIFTED HIMSELF UP. HE COULD NOT

TELL whether he had been asleep or not, but there in the lake he saw a wonderful sight: *the buffaloes!*

◈ There they were, hundreds and hundreds of them, rising out of the water. He could not see the surface anymore. Instead, he saw a lake of swaying bodies and heads that shook; and on their horns and tossing heads the water gleamed in the moonlight, as it had done in his dreams.

◈ Little Wolf felt the blood run along his body. He clutched at the prairie grass, crushing it in his hot hands. With staring eyes he drank in the great vision. And not only with his eyes but also with his ears and his nose: for his ears were filled with the trampling and snorting of the herd and the flash of the water as it moved under their hooves; and his nose inhaled the sharp moist smell of the great beasts as they crowded in on one another—the smell the wolves know well when it comes dropping down the wind.

◈ Little Wolf never knew what came to him, what spirit of the wild whispered in his ear; but suddenly he leaped to his feet and cried out. And when he cried, he flung his arms above his head. And then he cried out again.

◈ At the first cry, a shiver passed through the herd. As if they were one beast, the buffaloes threw up their heads and listened, absolutely still. Above the margin of the lake they saw, in the white light of the moon, a little wild boy making swift motions with his arms. He seemed to speak with his arms—to talk to them with the ripple of his muscles and the thrust of his fingers in the air. They had never seen such a thing before. Their eyes fastened on the boy excitedly, and shot out sparks of light. And when he cried out again, there swept through the stillness of the herd a stir, a movement, a ripple that Little Wolf could see. And the ripple became a wave, and the wave a swell. It was a swell of buffaloes that began on the outskirts of the herd and broke along the margin of the lake in a terrifying roar.

◈ It was a wonderful sound, that roar of the buffaloes on the edge of a stampede. It rolled far out on the prairie in the hollow silence of the night. Wandering wolves caught it, threw their long noses to the moon, and howled an answering cry.

IT WAS THE HOUR WHEN, ON THE LONELY PRAIRIE, SOUND

CARRIES an immense distance. But the ears it might have warned—the quick ears of Assiniboin warriors—did not catch it, for they were too far away on the northern trail.

◈ On moccasins noiseless as the padded feet of the wolves, as intent, and almost more cruel, these painted warriors were stealthily approaching the camp of Little Wolf's people, determined to wipe them out before the Dog Star faded in the dawn.

◈ But now the buffaloes had received the strange message that the Indian boy waved to them from the margin of the lake. Little Wolf did not understand this message. He had cried out to the buffaloes because he could not help himself, because he loved them as the creatures of his dreams. But when he saw and heard their answer, when they came surging out of the lake like a mighty flood, bellowing and stamping and tossing their heads, a wild excitement possessed him. For the first time in his life, he knew the meaning of fear.

◈ Swift as the wolf for whom he was named, he darted toward his pony. To unhobble it and leap upon its back took but a moment. Then he was off, riding for his life!

◈ Behind him came the terrible sound of the buffaloes as they swept out of the lake. Little Wolf threw a quick glance behind to see which way they took and saw the dark surging mass heave itself onto the prairie and gallop due north.

◈ Little Wolf tried to escape the middle rush of the herd by turning the pony's head slightly westward. Once the buffaloes surrounded him on all sides, he did not know what might happen. If the pony had been fresh, Little Wolf could easily have outstripped them, but after a long day the animal was tired, and was going at half its usual speed. Little Wolf again glanced over his shoulder. The buffaloes were gaining! He cried out to the pony—little, short cries that made a wild note in the night.

◈ As they swept along, the leaders of the left flank of the herd drew so close that Little Wolf could hear the snorting sound of their breath. Then they were beside him, and the pony and the buffaloes were galloping together. Yet they did nothing to harm him. They did not seem to have any other desire but to gallop on into the night.

◈ Soon Little Wolf was completely surrounded by the buffaloes. In front, behind, and on both sides of him, a heaving mass of buffaloes billowed like the sea. Again, as when he had cried out beside the lake, a wild feeling of excitement seized him, and he felt the blood stir along his scalp. And once again he shouted a cry—a long, ringing cry—flinging his arms above his head. And the buffaloes replied, bellowing a wild answer that rolled like thunder along the plains.

◈ Northward the great gallop swept—down the hollows, over the swells of the prairie, below the lonely ridges with their piles of stones that mark where Indians leave their dead. Crashing through the alder thickets beside the creeks and through the shallow creeks themselves, churning the water into a muddy foam, the mighty herd rolled on its way; and the thunder of its coming spread terror far and wide. The antelopes were off like the wind; the badgers and coyotes slunk into their holes. Even the wolves heeded the warning, vanishing shadowlike along the hollows to the east and west.

◈ Little Wolf was beside himself with excitement and joy. It seemed as if he, too, were a member of the herd, as if the buffaloes had adopted him and made him their own.

◈ Suddenly he saw something ahead. He could not see clearly because of the buffaloes in front of him, but it looked like a band of men. They were not mounted but were running swiftly on foot, as if to regain their ponies. At first, Little Wolf thought they were his own people; he knew by the outline of the country that the camp could not be far off. But then he saw that the men were not running toward the camp but away from it. Very swiftly, the thought flashed on him: They were Assiniboins, the deadly enemies of his tribe. They must have left their ponies some distance away in order to approach the camp unseen through the long grass and attack Little Wolf's people as they slept!

◈ Little Wolf knew well that unless his enemies reached their ponies in time, the buffaloes would cut off their retreat. Once that great herd hurled itself upon them, nothing could save them from being trampled. He saw the Assiniboins making desperate efforts to escape. He cried shrilly, hoping that it would excite the buffaloes even more. The buffaloes seemed to answer his cries. They bore down upon the fleeing men at a terrible gallop, never slackening speed. One by one the Assiniboins were overtaken, knocked down, and trampled underfoot.

◈ Suddenly, Little Wolf's pony went down too. The boy leaped clear as the animal fell. By this time they were on the outskirts of the herd, and before Little Wolf could get to his fallen pony, the last buffalo had passed. The pony struggled to its feet, trembling but unharmed, and with his arm around its neck, Little Wolf watched the herd disappear into the night...

Over the blazing campfires, when the wind moans eerily through the thickets of juniper and fir, they still speak of the great lake to the south where the buffaloes begin. But now they always add the name of Little Wolf to the legend, for he is the boy who led the buffaloes and saved his people.

———————————————— ◇◇◇ ————————————————